ADVENTURES ON FILE ISLAND

ADVENTURES ON FILE ISLAND

JOHN WHITMAN

HarperEntertainment
An Imprint of HarperCollinsPublishers

HarperEntertainment
An Imprint of HarperCollins*Publishers*
10 East 53rd Street, New York, NY 10022-5299

ISBN 0-06-107186-2

First printing: June 2000

Printed in the United States of America

Visit HarperEntertainment on the World Wide Web at www.harpercollins.com

❖ 10 9 8 7 6 5 4 3 2 1

Part One:
And So It Begins

If there was one thing Taichi "Tai" Kamiya liked better than summer camp, it was an afternoon *off* from summer camp. While the other kids played baseball or learned how to weave baskets, Tai snuck away to enjoy some downtime and the hot sun.

Leaving the campgrounds behind, Tai found a nice, wide tree branch and decided to relax for a while. Camp was cool, but sometimes Tai needed something a little different from the everyday routine.

Tai jumped up and grabbed the lowest tree branch, when he heard a voice behind him. "Hey, Tai, what are you doing?"

Tai looked over his shoulder and saw Sora Takenouchi. There weren't many camp kids as cool as Tai, but Sora was definitely one of them. Still swinging from the branch, Tai said, "Just hanging out." He pulled himself up onto the branch and stretched out. He could already feel the sun warming up his skin.

"Well, Matt and I are going down to the lake. You want to come?"

Tai thought about it for a minute. Yamato Ishida, whom everyone called Matt, was one of the most fun kids at summer camp. He was always good for a laugh, but Tai didn't feel like going. He'd been to the lake already that morning. He'd been to the lake yesterday, too. And the day before. And the day before that. This day just felt too normal to him. He wished something different would happen.

Little did he know, his wish was about to come true.

"No, thanks," Tai started to say. "I think I'll just–Hey!" He stopped, feeling something chilly touch his cheek. Brushing it away, he saw something soft and white on his fingers.

"What's wrong?" Sora asked.

"This looks like a . . . a snowflake," Tai said.

"Snow?" Sora asked doubtfully. "In the middle of July?"

But it *was* snowing. As the two kids looked upward, thick clouds covered the sun, and more snow began to fall.

A few other kids who'd been wandering nearby on their way to or from the lake stopped to look up. Tai recognized most of them. Matt was walking toward them, probably looking for Sora. But he stopped in surprise when the snow began to fall. On the porch of a nearby camp cottage, a fourth-grader named Koushiro "Izzy" Izumi sat poking away at his laptop computer. He had his nose so close to the screen he didn't even notice the snow piling on his head.

Mimi Tachikawa sat near the cottage picking pink flowers to match her pink dress. She stood up and held out her hands to catch a snowflake as another kid rushed by her—a little second-grader named Takeru Takaishi. Takeru, or "T.K.," was Matt's little brother.

Last but not least, Joe Kido stumbled out from behind a tree, looking like someone had just dropped an ice cube down his pants. Even though he was a sixth-grader and one of the oldest kids at summer camp,  Joe was the nervous type, and always had the surprised and startled expression of someone who wished he were somewhere else.

In seconds, the snowfall turned into a blizzard. Sheets of snow blew across the campgrounds, covering everything in white.

"Now that's a cold snap!" Tai said, shivering.

"We'd better get inside," Sora said.

"Let's try that cottage," Tai said.

They headed over to the cottage where Izzy was working at his computer. They arrived just as Matt showed up, pulling T.K.

along. The small group piled into the cottage. They were about to close the door when the others pushed their way inside. Finally Mimi and Joe hurried through the door.

"Brrrr, it's freezing!" Joe said. "Can we come inside?"

All seven kids stood inside the cottage watching the snow come down. But as quickly as it had begun, the snow stopped, leaving the ground covered by a cold, white blanket.

"What's going on with the weird weather?" T.K. asked.

Izzy looked up from his computer screen

for the first time. "It's happening all over the planet. Cities that are usually hot in the summer are now cold. In other places, it's snowing where it hasn't rained in months. I read about it on the Internet."

"I guess this means the canoe races at the lake are canceled," Sora said.

Tai shrugged. "So let's go sledding instead!"

He threw open the door and rushed outside, followed by Sora.

Joe Kido hesitated. "I worried about catching a summer cold," he said. "But this is ridiculous!"

Mimi stepped in front of him, smiling at the fresh, sparkling snow. "Wow! Let's make snow angels! I wish I'd brought my fluffy pink snowboots."

All the kids rushed outside into the

snow—except for little Izzy, who kept trying to get his computer link activated. The machine bleeped, and he groaned. "Still not working. Bummer. This storm's making a mess of my infrared Internet connection."

Outside, Tai looked up from the glistening snow to the sky, which was shining even more brightly. Even though clouds still hid the sun, an eerie, intense light was turning the sky different colors. Waves of blue and orange light streaked across the bottoms of the clouds.

"Hey, Izzy, come out! You gotta see this!" he called.

"Wow, it's beautiful," Mimi said. "Magical even."

"Yeah," Izzy said, joining the others. "But what is it?"

"I don't know," Joe said nervously. "But I think we all ought to get back inside before we catch pneumonia."

"And miss this?" Matt said. "This sky is, like, short-circuiting!"

As they watched, the beautiful lights grew brighter. Then a single dot of fiery light appeared. It grew brighter and larger, swirling around like a spinning ball of flame.

A moment later, the sky exploded.

Tai and the others threw their arms up protectively as the fireball flared up. Looking up through squinting eyes, Tai saw seven rays of light streaking toward the ground.

"Watch out!" he yelled. The light beams exploded at the feet of the seven kids, sending up a shower of snow and ice. The kids dove to the ground, covering their ears against the noise.

As the echoes of the explosions died away,  they all stood up again, wiping half-melted snow from their faces and hair. Despite the noise and fire, no one appeared to have been hurt.

"Is everyone all right?" Sora called out.

Matt helped his little brother to his feet. "We're still here."

"That was scary!" Mimi said breathlessly.

Joe was still trembling. "What was it?"

Izzy, who was smart for his age, or any age, scanned the snowy ground until he spotted a small hole. "This must be where one of those things hit. Maybe they were meteors."

He peered into the hole and saw something begin to glow faintly. The pale light suddenly rose up out of the hole and floated in the air. At the same time, little globs of light rose out of the other holes as well.

"I'm no rocket scientist," Matt said, "but I don't think meteors do this!"

Tai studied one of the little glowing objects. At its center was a small mechanical device about the size of his palm. Carefully, Tai reached out and grabbed hold of the mysterious object. At the same time, the other kids did the same. The lights vanished, and the children held in their hands small machines like tiny computers.

"What are they?" Tai asked.

Izzy studied one. "It looks like some sort of miniature digital apparatus," he said scientifically.

"With no instructions?" Joe asked nervously.

Tai heard something roar. Looking up, he could hardly believe what he saw. An enormous wall of water suddenly rose up out of the ground. Flecks of white foam splashed at the top of the wave a hundred feet above them. "Forget the instructions. Surf's up!" he yelled.

The enormous wall of water rolled toward them. It lifted the seven kids up and carried them high into the sky. Tai felt himself tossed and turned back and forth, rolling

and tumbling in the water until he could no longer tell which way was up. Just when he thought he could no longer hold his breath, he was pulled to the top of the wave. He gasped for breath.

Everything's going to be all right, he told himself, trying to calm his panicked heart. He'd been surfing before—this was just a really big wave. All they had to do was ride it out and they'd be fine.

But then Tai looked down and knew that this was no ordinary wave. Beneath them, the ground seemed to open up into a hole wider than the Grand Canyon. The water poured down into the hole with the sound of a hundred waterfalls, carrying Tai and the others with it. Tai felt himself falling down into the huge pit.

Then everything went black.

"Tai. Yoo-hoo, Tai!"

Tai was lying on his back on solid ground.

His eyes were still closed, but he felt warm sunlight on his skin again.

"Tai!" He heard his name again.

Tai opened his eyes and looked up.

And he found a pair of wide eyes staring down at

him. The eyes were attached to a basketball-sized blob with a big mouth and thin, floppy ears. The blob was sitting on his chest and smiling.

"Hello, Tai!"

"Yahhhh!" Tai shouted in alarm. He jumped up, throwing the creature off him and scrambling away. He was in the middle of a forest somewhere.

"Hey!" the creature said, bouncing toward him. "You don't need to be afraid of me. I'm your friend. I'm your friend!" The creature bounced around him excitedly.

Tai stared at the little creature for a

moment. He'd never seen an animal like it. It had no arms and no legs, and it *talked*. "Uh," he said, "just what are you? Have you had your rabies shots?"

The creature laughed. "Everything's going to be all right now. I've been waiting for you!" The little bouncing ball jumped into his arms.

"Waiting for me?" Tai asked.

"My name is Koromon! And we're partners."

"What does Koromon mean?" Tai asked. "Talking head?"

"It means brave little warrior, and don't forget it!" Koromon laughed again. "I am a Digimon, short for Digital Monster."

"How do you know my name?" Tai asked. "And what do you mean you were waiting for me?"

Something rustled in the underbrush, and Izzy appeared, still carrying his portable computer. "Tai?"

"Izzy!" Tai said.

"Yeah, it's me," Izzy said. "And I've got this little pink thing following me."

On cue, another small blob waddled into view. "Allow me to introduce myself. My friends call me Motimon!"

Izzy looked at Motimon. "I believe," he said, "that those digital devices we found have taken on digital life forms. I don't remember anything like this in the camp brochure."

"That's right!" Koromon said. "You're in the DigiWorld now!"

"And just where is the DigiWorld?" Tai asked.

Izzy said, "I don't so much care where it is as *what* it is."

Tai decided to have a look around for himself. He climbed a nearby tree to get a better view. At camp he'd been learning how to hike in the mountains, and he always carried a small spyglass with him. Now he pulled it out of his pocket and used it to look around.

He saw a forest stretch around him in all directions, with tall mountains rising up from the trees. Beyond the forest he saw a wide, blue ocean.

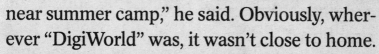

"There was no ocean near summer camp," he said. Obviously, wherever "DigiWorld" was, it wasn't close to home.

Koromon bounced up onto the branch next to him. "Hey, Tai, what do you see?"

Tai peered through his glass. "Nothing I recognize."

He tilted the spyglass up to the sky and saw something fly past. At first he thought it was a bird, except that it had too many legs. And its head was large . . . and it had huge jaws like scissors. Soaring across the sky, the creature roared.

"Look at that!" Tai said. As he spoke, the creature swerved so that its buglike face was in view. It grew larger by the second. "It's some sort of giant, red beetle," he said. "And it's heading right for us!"

Tai dropped the spyglass and saw the giant creature with his naked eye. It was even closer than he'd thought.

"Duck!" he yelled.

He pressed himself against the tree branch as the monster swooped down on him. Its huge jaws opened, then chomped down, snapping off the top of the tree like it

was a toothpick. Tai felt the wind rush by him as the monster hurtled past.

On the ground, Izzy yelled, "Watch out! It's coming around again!"

Beside him, Motimon said, "Ooh, that is one seriously bad Digimon even when he's in a good mood!"

Up in the tree, Koromon said, "That is Kuwagamon. He's an Insectoid Digimon. Vicious and ruthless! With teeth like knives and scissor-hands that can chop through anything!"

"No kidding!" Tai said. He saw the huge Digimon approach again, and this time there was no more tree to use as cover. "What are we going to do?"

Koromon didn't answer. Instead, he launched himself into the air. Gathering his strength, the little Digimon let loose a Bubble Blow. The tiny energy ball streaked toward Kuwagamon and burst against his head. The Bubble Blow didn't hurt Kuwagamon, but it startled him enough to make the giant Digimon swerve slightly off course. Kuwagamon still slammed into Koromon, sending the little monster spinning wildly into the trees. The tip of the

giant beetle's wings clipped Tai's tree, cutting the branch out from under him. Tai crashed to the ground in a heap of arms, legs, leaves, and twigs.

Izzy rushed forward. "Tai, are you okay?"

Tai groaned and stood up. "Well, I have had better days."

"Ooooooooh," they heard someone groan.

Tai saw little Koromon lying on the ground. The creature didn't appear to be injured, but he looked exhausted. "Hey, Koromon," he said, running over. "You should pick on bugs your own size." He held the small Digimon up in his hands. "You're pretty brave."

Koromon smiled. "It was nothing."

ROOOARRRRR! A terrifying bellow shook the sky.

"Here he comes again!" Izzy shouted.

They looked up and saw Kuwagamon coming around for another pass, his scissor-claws snapping together eagerly.

The other little Digimon, Motimon, bounced up and down. "In here!"

They followed him to the most unusual
tree Izzy and Tai had ever seen. It was blue
and sparkled with its own light. "In here!"
Motimon repeated.

With that, he jumped right into the tree
and disappeared.

Not knowing what else to do, the two
human boys followed him, and jumped forward. To their surprise, they passed right
through the bark of the tree as if it were a
curtain, and found themselves sitting inside
a tiny room.

Falling into the DigiWorld

"Hello, Tai!"

Digimons digivolve!

"Run!"

"Digimons, *attaaack*!!"

"Mimi! We took care of him, didn't we?"

Taking a plunge!

"Tomorrow's weather forecast calls for clear skies with occasional ice cream."

Tai gets all wound up.

"Agumon digivolve to . . .

. . . Greymon!"

"What kind of tree is this?" Izzy asked.

"It's a hiding tree, silly," Motimon answered.

They heard Kuwagamon roar above them, and then heard the *whoosh* of his wings as he passed overhead.

A moment later they heard another sound—one that was much more familiar.

"You can come out now!"

"Hey, that's Sora!" Tai said.

The two boys and their Digimon friends stepped out of the tree and back into the forest. There they found Sora waiting with

another of the strange little creatures. This one was a blob, like Koromon and Motimon, but it had several colorful stalks and flowers growing out of its head.

The new Digimon purred at them. "Enchanted to meet you. My name is Yokomon."

Sora smiled. "My own personal something-or-other."

"It looks kind of like a radish," Tai said.

Before anyone could speak, yet another of the Digimon creatures appeared. "Hello! I am Tokomon!"

"They're popping up everywhere!" Izzy said.

T.K. stepped through the bushes, followed by Matt, who was carrying another Digimon.

"Hey, Matt!" Tai said. "You, too?"

"Yeah, I'm here, too," Matt said.

"No, I mean that thing you're holding," Tai replied.

"Hello. You appear pleasant," said Matt's Digimon. Like the others, it was mostly blob, but it had a tall horn sticking out of its top. "My name is Tsunomon."

"Heeeellllpp! Heeeeellllllpp!"

They all jumped in surprise. Before they could react, Joe Kido exploded through the bushes, his eyes wide with fear. Behind him bounced a little dragon-like Digimon. "Help me! This thing won't leave me alone."

"I'm no thing! I'm Bukamon!" cried the little creature, bouncing happily into his arms.

Joe looked at his friends, who stood by calmly as the creature wriggled around in his arms. "What's wrong with you guys? Can't you see these ... these things?" He realized that no one else was nearly as frantic as he was, and started to calm down. "What ... what are they?"

All six creatures said at once: "We're Digimons. Digital monsters!"

Koromon added, "We're not just digital

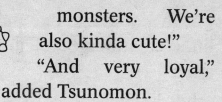

monsters. We're also kinda cute!"

"And very loyal," added Tsunomon.

Tai looked around and realized someone was missing. Everyone who had picked up one of those digital devices had been somehow transported to this strange island. Everyone, that was, except Mimi.

"Where do you think she is?" he asked once he'd pointed out she was missing. "She's bound to have come with us, don't you think?"

"Maybe she's off somewhere picking flowers," Joe suggested.

Just as he spoke, a scream filled the forest.

Instantly, they knew the scream had come from Mimi.

"Okay, so she's not picking flowers," Joe said.

Together, they raced toward the sound of a crying voice. As they entered a clearing they saw Mimi and a Digimon running for their lives. Huge Kuwagamon skimmed over the treetops, waiting for a chance to bite them.

"Everyone down!" Matt yelled. The entire group dropped to the dirt. Kuwagamon, unable to fly that low, passed overhead.

"This is the worst summer camp I've ever been to," Joe wailed. "My mom is going to want a total refund!"

Mimi, unable to speak, simply burst into tears. Her Digimon tried to comfort her.

"Don't worry, Mimi. Tanemon is here to protect you."

"Well, if we all want to be safe, we'd better move," Tai said.

The seven children and their Digimons hurried through the forest, looking for a safe place to hide. Although they couldn't see the sky through the thick layer of trees, they heard the buzz of Kuwagamon's wings and the roar of his voice in the sky above.

"I'm getting tired of running," Tai said. He didn't know where he was, but he *did* know that he didn't like being scared half out of his wits.

"There's no way we can fight that thing," Matt said.

"Not fight and win, anyway," Izzy agreed.

They kept running. A moment later, the trees ended unexpectedly, and the kids found themselves running across a short stretch of open ground. That ground, too, ended sharply—in a cliff overlooking the ocean. The group pulled up short.

"Oh, great." Matt groaned. "Anyone have a helicopter?"

Tai was determined not to give up. He carefully moved to the edge of the cliff and looked down. Two hundred feet below, a river flowed past the face of a sheer cliff wall. "There's no way down," he said.

He turned back to the others just in time

to see the trees behind them shake, and then suddenly vanish as Kuwagamon cut through them like a lawn mower. Once more the kids ducked, barely avoiding the Digimon's slashing jaws. Kuwagamon rose into the air, then curved around for another pass. The creature headed straight for the closest target: Tai.

Standing at the edge of the cliff, Tai had nowhere to run. Beside him, he felt the little Digimon begin to tremble as though gathering his energy.

"Here I go!" Koromon shouted.

Once again, the little Digimon launched himself into the air. He let loose another Bubble Blow, which blasted against the side of Kuwagamon's red shell. But this time it wasn't enough to stop Kuwagamon. The huge Digimon brushed Koromon aside and contin-

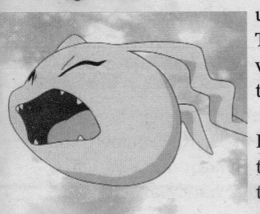

ued straight ahead. Tai leaped out of the way, barely dodging the snapping jaws.

Without slowing, Kuwagamon changed targets and swooped toward the rest of the group.

"Digimons, attack!" shouted the six remaining creatures. The small Digimons leaped into the air, each one letting loose a Bubble Blow. Combined, the energy blasts had more power as they smashed into Kuwagamon's face. The big Digimon roared and lost its balance, spinning off course and crashing into the trees. The monster disappeared from sight among the branches and leaves.

The kids waited a moment, but there was no sound. For the moment, at least, Kuwagamon had been defeated.

Sora was the first to turn and look for the small Digimons. She saw them all lying on the ground, exhausted. "Yokomon!" she called out.

The kids rushed toward their newfound friends. Tai picked up Koromon. The poor creature looked small and weak. "Are you crazy? Why did you do it?" Tai asked.

"Sorry," Koromon said in a small voice. "It's just that I'm trying to make a good impression."

"They must be programmed for courage," Izzy guessed.

All of the rest of the Digimons were unconscious, spent by their short battle with the giant Kuwagamon. "Bukamon, wake up," Joe pleaded, but neither Bukamon nor the other Digimons stirred.

ROOOOARRRRR!

The sound of Kuwagamon's voice filled the air once more. The giant Digimon had recovered from the attack and was about to charge again.

Picking up their Digimons, the young friends backed away from the trees. But they could only go a short distance before

they reached the edge of the cliff.

Tree trunks snapped and branches fell to the ground as Kuwagamon, no longer flying, stepped forward. Each step that he took made the ground tremble. Standing on his massive hind legs, Kuawagamon was at least two stories tall. His huge scissor-hand jaws snapped together.

Tai felt his heart pound in his chest. "Okay, get ready to run."

But in his arms, Koromon stirred. "No, don't run. Fight!"

"Give it up, will you?" Tai said.

Motimon's eyes popped open. "Koromon's right. It's time that we show what we're made of."

Sora looked at the Digimons, who were all still weak from the first battle. "But you're no match for him!"

By now, all the Digimons had reawakened, and all of them were struggling to break free of the hands that held them. "Lemme go, lemme go, lemme go!" Tsunomon yelled.

As one, the little Digimons slipped from the arms of the children and hurled themselves at Kuwagamon.

"No!" Tai cried. "You'll be killed!"

5

Tai felt a pit open in his stomach, deeper than the one that had dropped them into the DigiWorld. He'd only known Koromon for a short time, but already he admired the little creature's great courage. For such a small creature, Koromon had a huge heart. If only there were something he could do to help!

As he thought those words, Tai felt the digital device he'd put in his pocket start to grow warm. Then it flashed brightly. At the same time, all the devices his friends carried flashed, too.

As the devices activated, they seemed to summon great beams of light from the sky itself. The light beams shot downward upon the seven tiny Digimons, filling them with new energy.

Koromon stopped in his tracks. Suddenly, the little creature called out, "Koromon digivolve to . . . Agumon!"

The energy beam washed over him, and the Digimon morphed into something larger and tougher, a lizardlike creature with sharp claws and powerful jaws.

One by one, the other Digimons transformed as well.

"Yokomon digivolve to . . . Biyomon!" The little blob turned into a birdlike creature.

"Motimon digivolve to . . . Tentomon!" A quick-legged bug appeared and buzzed its wings, rising eagerly into the air.

45

"Tsunomon digivolve to . . . Gabumon!" The tiny horn-headed blob was replaced by a striped blue creature with fur and flippers.

"Tokomon digivolve to . . . Patamon!" The small blob transformed into a larger monster with legs and long ears.

"Bukamon digivolve to . . . Gomamon!" The dragonlike Digimon changed into a creature like a sharp-clawed sea animal.

"Tanemon digivolve to . . . Palmon!" Mimi's Digimon transformed into a tall plant-like creature.

As the weird energy beams faded, seven larger, tougher Digimons squared off against Kuwagamon. "What happened to the little guys?"

Mimi asked aloud.

The seven Digimons charged. But Kuwagamon was still larger than all of them put together. With one swipe of his claw, he knocked them all backward into the dirt. At first Tai thought the massive creature's claw had torn them apart. But the seven Digimons were tough, and they popped back onto their feet immediately.

"All right then," Agumon growled. "You asked for it!"

Kuwagamon, realizing he had a fight on his hands, flapped his wings to lift off. But

Palmon jumped forward and raised her hands. "Poison ivy!" she shouted.

Long tendrils like roots shot out and wrapped themselves around Kuwagamon's legs, holding him down.

At the same time, Patamon leaped into the air, crying "Boom Bubble!" as he let loose a powerful energy ball that blasted the red beetle off balance.

The digivolved monsters did not let up. Tentomon followed the attack with a shot of his Electrical Super Zapper. Seeing an opening, Gamamon rolled forward, knocking one of Kuwagamon's legs out from under him.

"Stand back, everyone!" Agumon said. The Digimon filled his lungs with air. "Pepper Breath!"

Agumon blew a blast of fire that scorched the red beetle's face. Gabumon followed it up immediately with an icy shot of his Blue Blaster, and Biyomon added her Spiral Twister that curved toward Kuwagamon. The combination of blows stunned the giant Digimon, and it roared.

"Now, all together!" Agumon yelled.

The Digimons gathered themselves and

fired. All their weapons combined to slam into Kuwagamon. Fire and energy exploded against the beetle's chest, throwing him off his feet and slamming him backward into the trees again.

The seven humans were stunned. "Amazing," Tai whispered. Then he ran forward. "Koromon! Or Agumon, or whoever you are. You did it!"

He threw himself into Agumon's arms. The entire group cheered.

But their celebration came too soon.

Kuwagamon was a champion among

Digimons, and he could not be so easily defeated. The monster leaped quickly to its feet. Angrily, it smashed full-grown trees out of its way and lunged forward again. But this time he didn't attack the monsters or the humans themselves. Using his massive scissor-hands, Kuwagamon attacked the cliff itself. The blades of his jaws sank into the ground, cracking the stone.

"Look out!" Sora cried, but it was too late.

The cliffside broke away and plunged toward the river below, taking the humans and Digimons with it.

Part Two:
The Birth of
Greymon

6

Once again, Tai felt himself falling. But this time it wasn't into a strange new world. He was plunging down toward a river, with a ton of rock falling all around him.

As he fell, Tai caught a glimpse of some of the Digimons, like Patamon and Tentomon, grabbing hold of the humans and trying to fly, slowing their fall. Palmon used some of her limbs to grab Mimi, and the rest to shoot long tendrils up to the rocks. But the Digimons were still too small to hold the larger humans, and all of them continued to fall.

Tai saw the water rush up at him and did his best to straighten his body, the way he did when he jumped off the high-dive at the public swimming pool. He closed his eyes, held his breath, and hit the water with a splash. For a moment he was blinded by the water, but he heard and felt the others splash around him.

Tai kicked his way to the surface and coughed water out of his lungs. He started to dog-paddle to stay afloat . . . and only then did he realize how tired he was. Getting swept up by a mysterious tidal wave, running through the forest, being chased by a giant beetle, and falling off a cliff had sapped his strength.

"Tai!"

He realized Sora was next to him, dog-paddling as well.

"You okay, Sora?" he asked.

"I'm . . . not sure . . . how long I can swim," Sora gasped.

"Me . . . too."

Nearby, Tai saw Gomamon, the monster who'd been called Bakumon until he'd "digivolved," rise up in the water. The little creature shouted, "Marching Fishes!"

What happened next was one more amazing event in a day full of wonders. Out of nowhere, fish appeared. Not dozens of fish, or even hundreds, but *thousands* of fish. Fish swimming around them, fish swimming under them—so many fish that in moments, Tai and the others were lifted up out of the water. They were lying on a bed of fish all wriggling and squirming beneath them.

"Wow, this is some ride," he muttered.

ROOOARRRR!

The sound of Kuwagamon's battle cry shook the air above them.

"Doesn't he ever give up?" Matt wondered aloud.

Looking up, they saw the giant beetle standing on the cliff's edge, looking down at them. But Kuwagamon had forgotten his own tricks. The cliff on which he stood was already weak because of the section he chopped away. The rest of the stone couldn't bear his huge weight. As the creature stared

down at its targets, the rest of the cliff gave way, and the huge Digimon suddenly plummeted down.

"Look out!" Tai yelled.

"Go!" shouted Gomamon.

As quick as a thought, the thousands of fish all started swimming together, carrying the humans and Digimons across the water at a high speed. In a few short seconds they'd cleared out from beneath Kuwagamon and were a hundred yards away.

Kuwagamon hit the water with an enormous splash; a splash that sent waves high into the air. Gomamon urged his fish friends on, but one of the waves still caught up to them. The wave lifted the Digimons, the humans, and the fish into the air and tossed them forward, onto the banks of the river.

For a while the whole group, humans and Digimons alike, just lay on the shore without moving. Tai felt as if his entire body was bruised. All he wanted to do was sleep. But they still didn't know where they were, or how they'd arrived, or what these creatures were, and finally his curiousity got the best of him.

He sat up and looked around. At the same time, the others also began to stir.

Joe sat up and mumbled, "What was that? A floating fish-market?"

Gomamon laughed. "Those fish are just friends of mine. I just asked them for a lift, that's all."

Joe pushed his glasses up on his nose.

"And all these years I thought I was allergic to seafood. Thank you, um, I guess it's not Bukamon now?"

"Nope. It's Gomamon now!"

T.K. looked at the Digimon who'd become his friend. "So you're not Tokomon, are you?"

"Now I'm Patamon!" said the little Digimon.

Agumon snorted and looked at Tai. "It's all because we digivolved."

"I don't think that word's in my dictionary," he replied.

But Izzy, whose mind worked like a computer, had already figured out the process. "So digivolving is what they do when they advance to the next level and become more powerful."

"No kidding," Tai said. He looked at Agumon. "When you digivolved you got way bigger.

Does this mean you're still a Digimon, or something different?"

"Digimon!" Agumon laughed. "Just stronger than before. But I needed your help, Tai."

"Help with what?"

"You see," the Digimon said, "digivolving is a very difficult process. I had to share your energy."

Sora looked at Biyomon, the birdlike Digimon who had become her friend. "I guess you guys don't run on batteries."

"Sure don't!" the bird Digimon said.

Izzy studied his Digimon friend, Tentomon.

"But how do you access my energy?" he asked.

The Insectoid Digimon shrugged. "Even we don't know everything," Tentomon replied.

Palmon danced around Mimi, laughing. "Thanks for my magical powers."

But the girl in pink just put her head in her hands. "The whole thing makes my head spin."

Joe looked skeptical. "Hmm, my mother warned me about strangers."

Gomamon laughed. "I'm not a stranger, Joe, I'm your friend for life."

The humans all looked at one another and had the same thought. *Friends for life? What have we gotten into?*

7

Matt was growing a little impatient with all the small talk. But he didn't want to lose his cool, so he said as casually as he could: "Okay, so what are we going to do now?"

Joe said, "If only there was a pay phone nearby. We could call the police or the fire department, or my mother."

"We should go exploring," Tai said. "And find our way around."

Izzy scanned the forest around them. "But we're not sure where to go. We don't even have a compass to tell us which way is north."

His Digimon friend, Tentomon, laughed. "I know where north is."

"You do?" Izzy asked. "Where?"

"It's the opposite of south!"

"Ah," Izzy said sarcastically. "That's helpful."

Joe didn't care if they had a compass or not. "I'm not *exploring* anywhere."

Matt sighed. "Right, we can just stay here and wait for that monster to find us. We need to find a road that leads away from here."

"You know," Sora said, using her brain, "if we could get back to where we were before, we might find a way out of here."

"But wait!" Mimi said worriedly. "Are there more monsters around like that Kuwagamon?"

"Oh, yes, indeed," said Palmon.

"Those monsters don't scare me," said Matt coolly.

Tai turned to Agumon. "Are there more humans in this place?"

"Humans?" the reptile Digimon replied. "There's never been anything but Digimons."

"And these monsters are all Digimons, too?"

"Yep, that's right."

"What do we do when it gets dark?" Sora asked.

"Who says it ever gets dark here?" Matt pointed out.

Izzy frowned. "That phenomenon would be unnatural."

Joe snorted. "And you call this natural? We don't even know what this place is!"

Agumon said, "You're in DigiWorld. This place is called File Island."

Matt shook his head. "Yeah, that helps. Now I know exactly where we are."

Tai decided there'd been enough talking. "Well, we're not going to find out anything standing here. I'm going."

"Where?" Matt asked.

"Back up to that cliff. That's where I saw the ocean." The boy started walking up the river. "Maybe we can find a boat or something."

"A boat?" Matt said. "Yeah, maybe we can water-ski home."

Joe shook his head. "At a time like this I think we'd all be better off just finding a cave and hiding. We can keep our eyes open and ... um ..." He looked up and realized that everyone else had started following Tai.

Joe sighed and grumbled, "I should have worn different pants. These ride up when I walk too much."

● ● ●

The group walked along the edge of the river. As they did, the humans looked around at the fantastic world into which they'd fallen. In some ways it looked normal—there were trees, and a river, and mountains. But the trees were like none they'd ever seen, and the sky seemed to go from cloudy to clear at a moment's notice.

Izzy, who was fascinated by machines, couldn't take his eyes off the Digimons. "You say that you're digital monsters," he said to Tentomon. "But you don't look like machines to me."

"Oh, yeah?" Tentomon replied. "Watch this!"

Tentomon's eyes narrowed, and an electrical spark jumped between his antennae with a *zap!*

They walked on for a short time before reaching the end of the river. But instead of leading them back to the cliffs, the water led them straight to the ocean Tai had seen.

As they reached the beach, they heard the last sound they expected to hear. It was a telephone ringing. Hurrying over a sand dune, they saw a string of telephone booths

lined up right near the water's edge. It was strange enough to see telephone booths on the beach . . . but what was even stranger was the number of telephones. They seemed to stretch on and on into the distance.

Telephone booths in the middle of nowhere—and one of them was ringing!

Tai sprinted forward. "We're saved!" he yelled. But by the time he reached the phone, the ringing had stopped.

"Does anyone have any loose change?" he asked.

"Call collect," Matt suggested. "And, hey, if you find a place that delivers, order us a pizza!"

Tai punched in his home phone number. The phone rang, and someone answered. "Hi, Mom?" he started to say.

But the voice that came on sounded like a recording. All it said was, "At the tone the time will be . . . forty-five miles per hour and ninety seconds."

"What?" Tai said in surprise. "Either

that's a wrong number or Mom's flipped."

The next time he called, the recording was even more ridiculous.

"Today's weather calls for clear skies and occasional ice cream."

He tried a third time, and the recording said, "This phone number exists only in your imagination. Please hang up and don't call back."

Tai hung up the phone. "Weird."

He was tempted to try another phone, and another, but something told him that every time he did, he'd only get the same sort of nonsense. He and the others gave up quickly, but Joe kept trying phone after phone.

"I think staying around here is a waste of time," Tai concluded.

Matt frowned. "But even if we can't call out, someone might be able to call us. Besides, I think we could all use a rest."

Tai looked at the others. They were all exhausted. "And I'm hungry, too," said Izzy.

"Does anyone have anything to eat?" Tai asked.

The seven kids started going through their belongings to see what they had. All of them still had the little digital devices that had crashed into the earth just before their adventure began, but other than that they didn't have much.

Tai had only his spyglass. Izzy had his laptop computer, a digital camera, and his cell phone—but not a single one of them had worked since they'd arrived in the DigiWorld. Sora hada first-aid kit, but nothing else. Matt, too, was empty-handed.

Little T.K. stepped forward, smiling. "Look what I've got!" He opened his backpack to reveal piles of cookies and chips. They were all hungry, but all of them knew that eating those snacks on an empty stomach would just make them sick.

Sora looked at Mimi's big bag. "What have you got in there, Mimi, cosmetics and hairbrushes?"

Mimi sighed. "Well, let's see." She started pulling things out of the bag. "I've got a compass, cooking fuel, a flashlight, a Swiss Army knife, and some other stuff."

Everyone's jaws dropped. Who'd have thought that little Mimi would be so prepared?

"Why didn't you tell us you had a compass?" Tai asked.

"I thought it would be fun to see how far we could get without one," Mimi laughed. "Besides, it's broken."

Matt said, "But we could use the cooking fuel to light a signal fire."

"That's true," Sora said grumpily, "or I guess we could barbecue some telephones."

Tai glanced over at the phones where Joe was still trying to call home. He noticed the bag Joe was carrying, and gasped. "Hey, Joe's got the emergency kit! Hey, Joe!"

Joe looked up from the phone. "Don't you know it's rude to—"

"Listen!" Tai said. "You've got food!"

A few moments later they had opened the emergency kit and divided up the food.

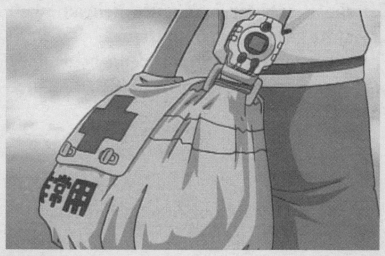

Planning carefully, they decided they had enough food to last for three days. The Digimons said they could forage for themselves.

The kids ate their first snack right away. "Here, Agumon, have a bite," Tai said. "I know you can find your own food, but you might as well have some of mine right now."

"Thanks, Tai!" the Digimon said, gobbling down a bite of food.

Biyomon suddenly turned and stared out at the beach for a minute. Beneath their feet, the ground began to tremble.

"What's wrong?" Sora asked.

Biyomon said softly, "Trouble."

Plumes of water suddenly shot up from the sand as though something was pushing the water up out of the ground. Water spouts blasted up through a whole row of telephone booths, sending them flying into

the air. A few yards away from the group, the ground began to rise up like a bubble.

"Scatter!" Tai yelled.

The humans and the Digimons backed away as something sharp and spinning pushed up through the ground. It looked like a giant drill with spikes attached.

"Uh-oh," said Tentomon. "It's Shellmon."

"What's Shellmon?" Izzy asked.

"Something that gets mad for no reason."

The creature certainly *looked* mad. As it rose out of the ground, a huge reptile head and feet poked out from a hole in the spike-covered shell. The shell was taller than a building, and Shellmon's head rose even higher into the sky. Atop its head, a bunch of snakelike tentacles wriggled. Spotting the group, Shellmon let loose an angry roar.

Using his powerful front legs, Shellmon dragged his shell forward.

"Run!" Joe said. He started to climb a steep sand dune nearby. Shellmon lowered his lizardlike head. From a spout in the top,

a powerful stream of water shot forward, slamming into the boy and making him fall back to the ground.

Agumon growled. "Digimons, attack!" he cried.

Together, the Digimons charged.

"Pepper Breath!" Agumon cried, releasing a Fireball. The blast struck Shellmon in the face, driving him back.

"Blue Blaster!" Gabumon said. He launched a Blue Blast, but the energy beam fizzled out before it reached the target.

"Spiral Twister!" Biyomon called. Her own weapon started to spin, but it, too, died before it could strike Shellmon. Tentomon tried to attack, but he couldn't muster enough strength to let loose his Super Shocker.

"What's happening to them?" Izzy asked.

"They look like they've lost their power!" Matt said.

Shellmon released another water blast

that swept all the Digimons off their feet. The Digimons looked too weak to stand up—all except Agumon, who leaped to his feet immediately.

"Go get him, Agumon!" Tai cheered.

The reptile Digimon dashed forward and released another blast of Pepper Breath that scorched Shellmon's face. The big Digimon backed up for a moment, then shook its head and started forward with a growl.

"Why is it only Agumon?" Izzy wondered.

Tentomon gasped, "We're just too weak from hunger."

"That's it," Sora said. "Agumon's the only one who had something to eat."

Tai looked at his Digimon friend. "Looks like it's just you and me, Agumon!"

"Then give me a diversion!" the monster called.

Tai dashed forward. "Hey, ugly, over here!"

As the huge monster turned toward Tai, Agumon let loose another blast of Pepper Breath. But Shellmon ignored it. He leaned toward Tai and one of the tentacles on his head wrapped itself around the boy's waist, lifting him high into the air.

"Tai!" yelled Agumon. But Shellmon raised one huge paw and brought it down on the smaller Digimon, pinning him to the ground.

Keeping those two trapped, the monster was free to attack the others. Shellmon let loose yet another Water Blast that pounded the remaining humans and Digimons to the ground.

Tai struggled to break free, pulling and scratching at the thick tentacle that held

him. "He's going to get everyone, and there's nothing I can do!"

Held high in the air by the tentacle, Tai looked down. Far below, Agumon was pinned down by Shellmon's paw. Tai felt a mixture of anger and guilt. He'd tried to help Agumon fight, but he'd only ended up getting caught. If only there were some way he could free the brave little Digimon!

His thoughts seemed to trigger the digi-vice he still kept hooked to his belt. It flashed brightly, sending out a beam of powerful energy that streaked toward Agumon, filling him with a glow-ing light. Agumon's eyes flashed, and he shouted, "Agumon digivolve to . . . *Greymon*!"

Instantly, the little Digimon began to change. He grew ten times taller, and much broader and stronger, with the body of a giant lizard, but with long, sharp horns on his head. He shrugged off Shellmon's paw easily, throwing the other Digimon off balance. Startled, the Evil Digimon dropped Tai to the ground. The cute face of Agumon was gone. Although he didn't look nearly as mean as Shellmon, this new Digimon looked every bit as tough.

"Wow!" Tai said, scrambling to his feet. "Agumon is now Greymon!"

The two giant Digimons squared off, growling at one another. Then, with a roar,

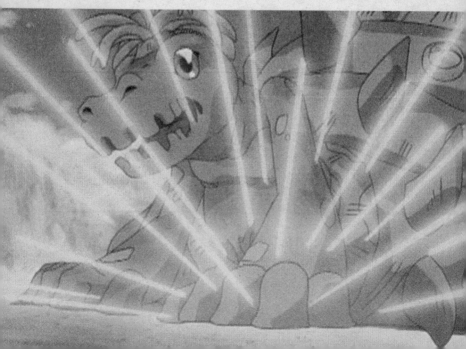

Shellmon charged forward, trying to drive Greymon off his feet. Bracing himself, Greymon caught the other monster by the head and stopped his charge. Greymon's powerful claws dug into the ground and his muscles strained to hold Shellmon back.

"Come on, Greymon!" Tai cheered.

Shellmon lowered his head, putting his water spout right in Greymon's face, and fired. The powerful water blast smashed right into Greymon's face, nearly throwing him off his feet. But bravely he held on. The Digimon gathered himself and fired his Flaming Breath. The fire was so hot it turned Shellmon's water to steam. Surprised, Shellmon stepped back.

That gave Greymon the space he needed. Dropping his head, he used his horns to scoop Shellmon off the ground. With a flick of his powerful head and neck, Greymon hurled the other monster high into the air.

Greymon's sharp eyes watched Shellmon fly through the air as he yelled, "Nova Blast!"

With a roar, he released an immense ball of fire that scorched the air. The Fireball streaked toward Shellmon and struck him squarely on the stomach, igniting with the force of an exploding sun. It struck Shellmon in midflight and launched him even higher, sending him far out to sea where he landed with a splash.

Greymon watched him fall. As soon as Shellmon had disappeared, the huge creature's body flashed with light and instantly shrank back into the much smaller Agumon. Once he was finished morphing, Agumon collapsed to the ground.

9

Tai sprinted forward and fell to his knees beside Agumon. "Are you all right?"

Agumon raised his head weakly. "Tai, do you have . . . anything to eat?"

A short time later the kids and the Digimons were gathered together, with the humans feeding their Digimons anything and everything they wanted to eat.

As the Digimons gobbled food, Tai looked around at the tele- phones that had been destroyed by Shellmon. "There's

really no reason to stay around here now."

Izzy nodded. "And Shellmon wasn't destroyed. We should move before he comes back."

"In that case, let's go back where we were before," Joe said. "If anyone's looking for us, that's where they'll be."

Sora sighed. "Joe, we fell off a cliff and

went down a river to get here. Getting back would be a very big job."

"Now, listen," said Izzy, always using his brain. "Logically speaking, if there are phones here, there must be people to use them. So I think it makes good sense to try to find those people."

Tai nodded. "Then let's all get going."

Agumon jumped to his feet. "Anywhere you want to go, I'll go, Tai. Just lead the way."

"Then let's get out of this place!" the boy said.

Matt said, "And let the monsters beware!"

Joe gulped. "Um, my plan is to avoid all monsters."

"I don't think we have much choice, Joe," Tai said.

He looked around at this strange new world. He wanted to go home as much as the others did, but he also felt a powerful sense of adventure. They were in a world possibly without other humans. They had made friends with strange, talking creatures

that were cute and cuddly, but also full of incredible power. Who could say what great adventures lay ahead?

Tai smiled, thinking back to the morning when he'd wished for something different. He'd certainly gotten what he asked for.

Tai looked at the others and nodded. "Okay, let's go."

The monsters leaped to their feet and all cried out at once, "Digimon!"